26 letters and 99 cents

BY TANA HOBAN

GREENWILLOW BOOKS
An Imprint of HarperCollinsPublishers

This one is for Candace

Soft Touch letters and numbers used in this book are available
at most toy stores or through International Playthings Inc.,
116 Washington Street, Bloomfield, NJ 07003.

The photographs were reproduced from 35-mm slides
and printed in full-color.

Manufactured in China
First Edition 24 23 22

Library of Congress Cataloging-in-Publication Data

Hoban, Tana. 26 letters and 99 cents.
"Greenwillow Books."
Summary: Color photographs of letters, numbers,
coins, and common objects introduce the alphabet,
coinage, and the counting system.
1. English language—Alphabet—Juvenile literature.
2. Counting—Juvenile literature. [1. Alphabet.
2. Counting. 3. Coins] I. Title.
II. Title: Twenty-six letters and ninety-nine cents.
PE1155.H57 1987 [E] 86-11993
ISBN 0-688-06361-6 (trade). ISBN 0-688-06362-4 (lib. bdg.)
ISBN 0-688-14389-X (paperback).

A a

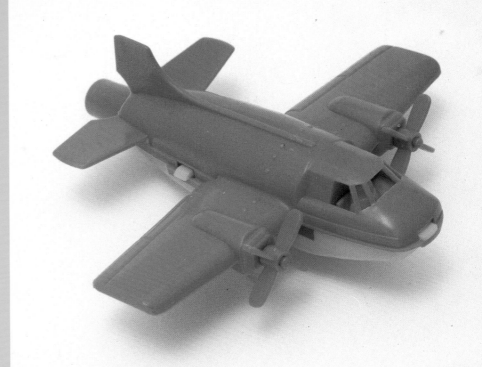

B b

C c

D d

Ee

Ff

Gg

Hh

Kk

Ll

Mm

Nn

O o

P p

Qq

Rr

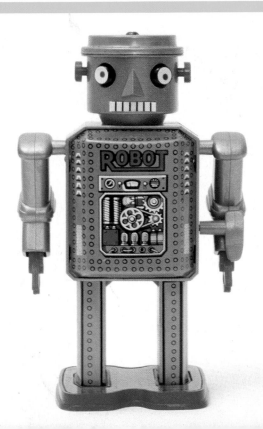

S s

T t

Uu

Vv

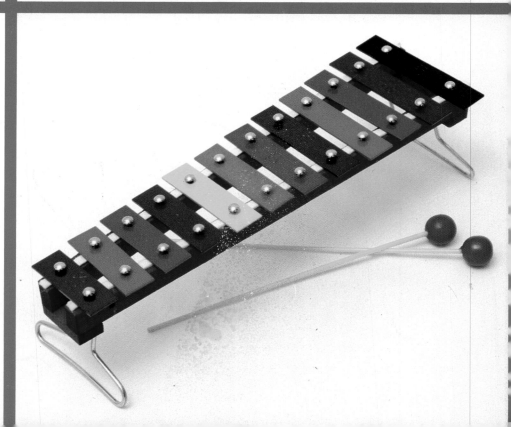

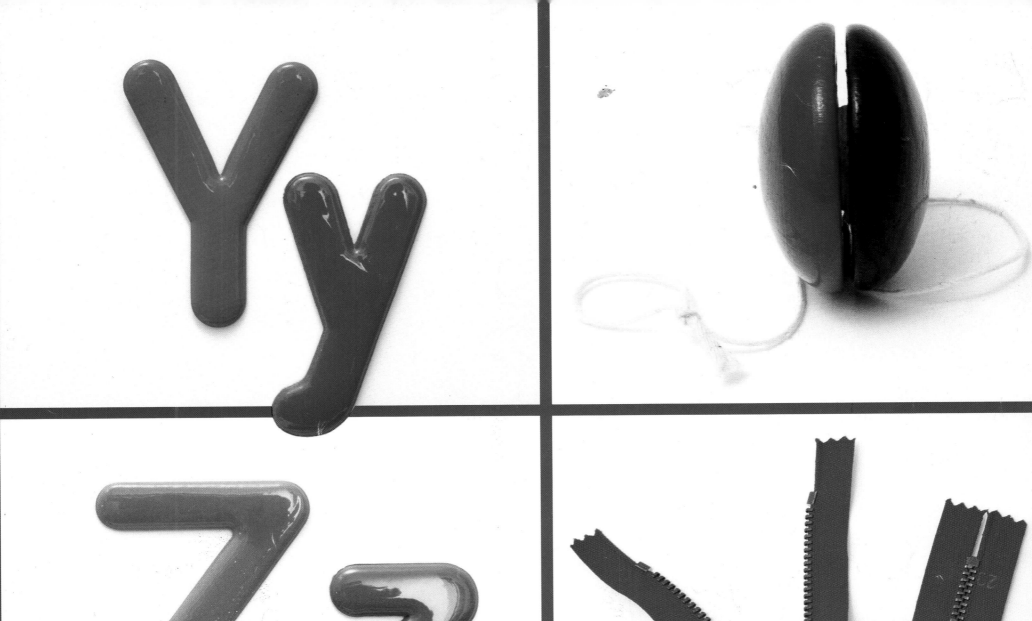

Yy

Zz

TURN THE BOOK AROUND FOR 99 cents

60

80

70

90

99

TURN THE BOOK AROUND FOR 26 letters

27		35	
28		40	
29		45	
30		50	

21

22

15

16

13

14

11

12

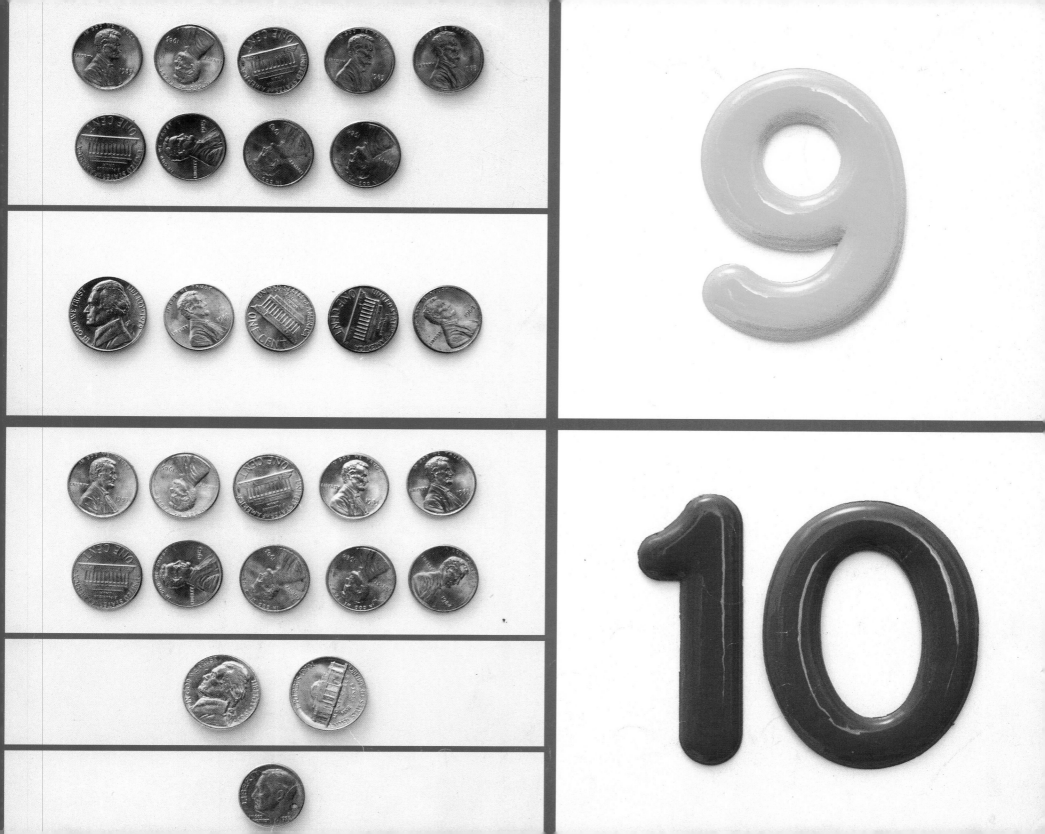

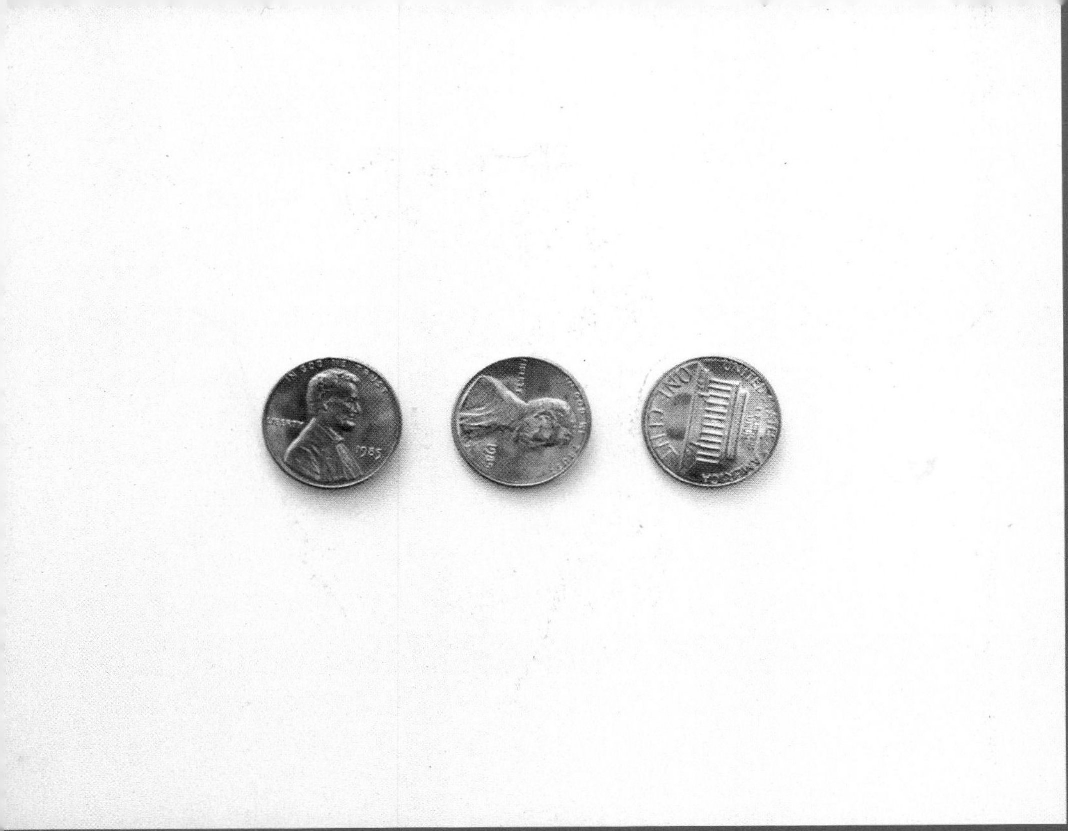

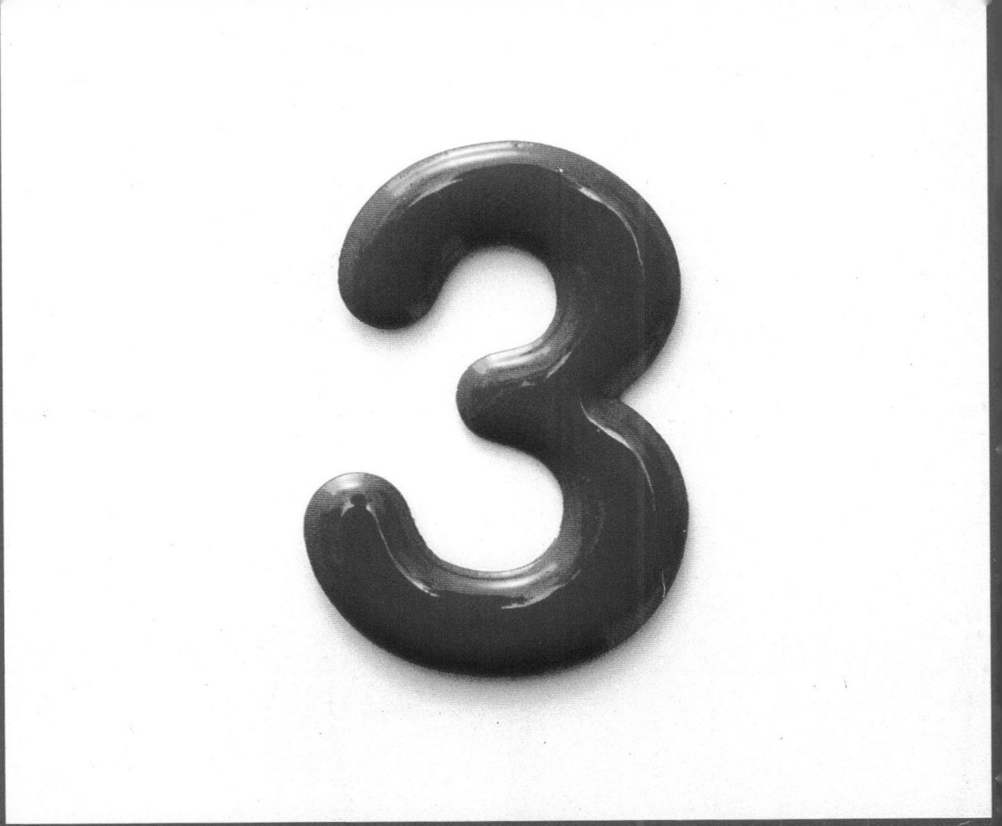
3

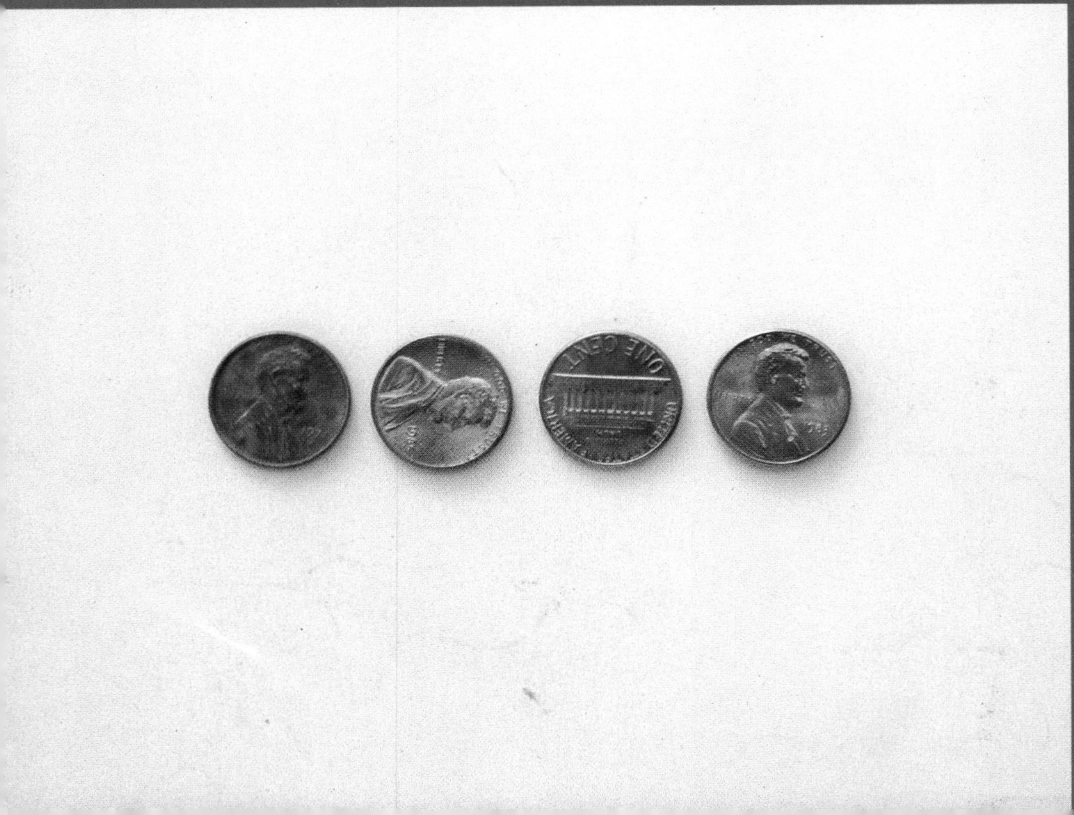

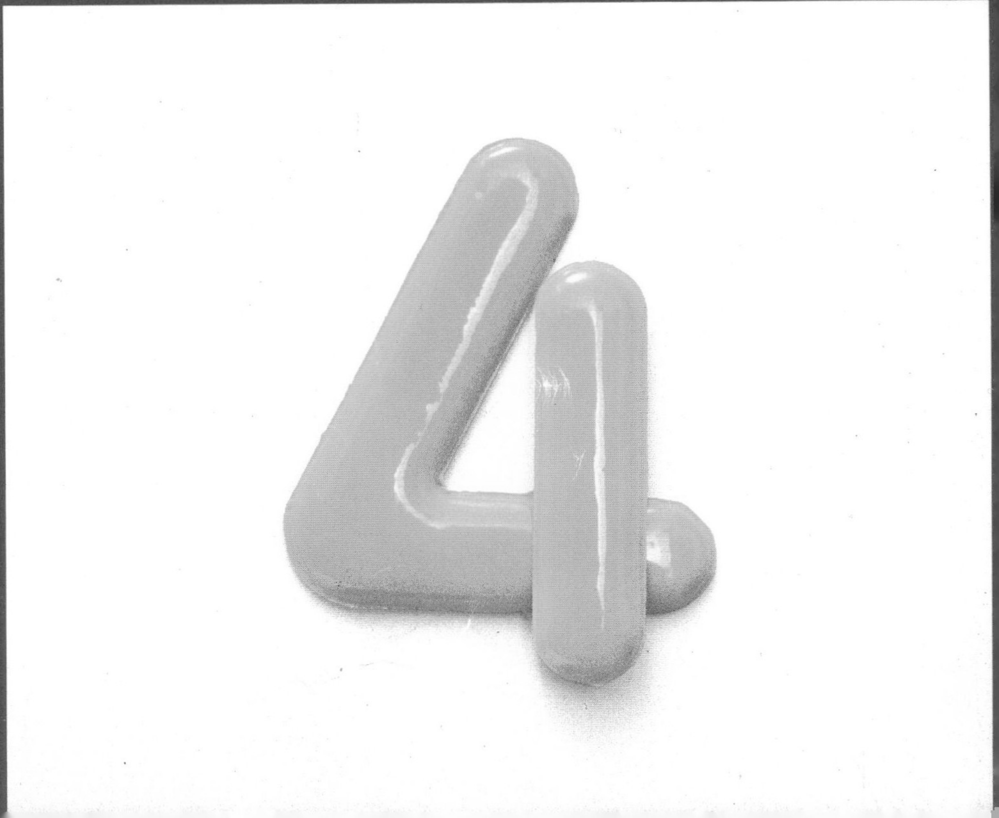
4

This one is for Candace

Soft Touch letters and numbers used in this book are available
at most toy stores or through International Playthings Inc.,
116 Washington Street, Bloomfield, NJ 07003.

The photographs were reproduced from 35-mm slides
and printed in full-color.

Manufactured in China
First Edition 24 23 22

Library of Congress Cataloging-in-Publication Data

Hoban, Tana. 26 letters and 99 cents.
"Greenwillow Books."
Summary: Color photographs of letters, numbers,
coins, and common objects introduce the alphabet,
coinage, and the counting system.
1. English language—Alphabet—Juvenile literature.
2. Counting—Juvenile literature. [1. Alphabet.
2. Counting. 3. Coins] I. Title.
II. Title: Twenty-six letters and ninety-nine cents.
PE1155.H57 1987 [E] 86-11993
ISBN 0-688-06361-6 (trade). ISBN 0-688-06362-4 (lib. bdg.)
ISBN 0-688-14389-X (paperback).

26 letters and 99 cents

BY TANA HOBAN

GREENWILLOW BOOKS
An Imprint of HarperCollinsPublishers

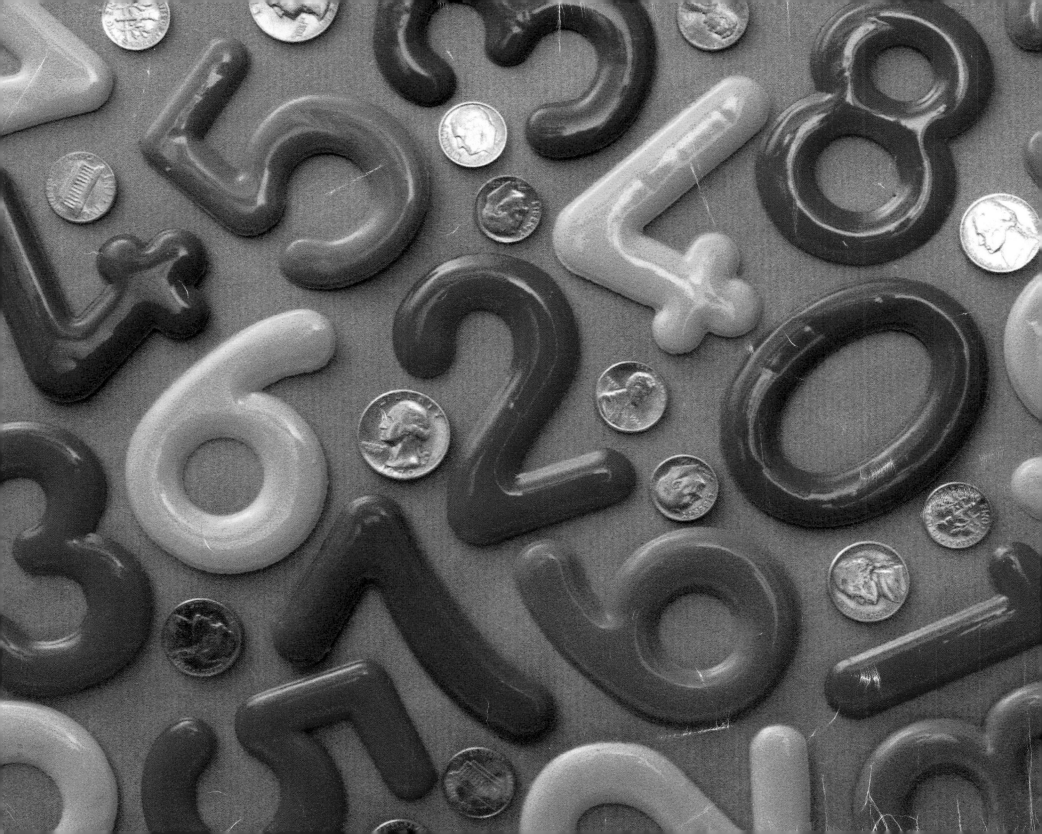